Flex
and the Fix-it Day

Illustrations by Niall Harding

EGMONT

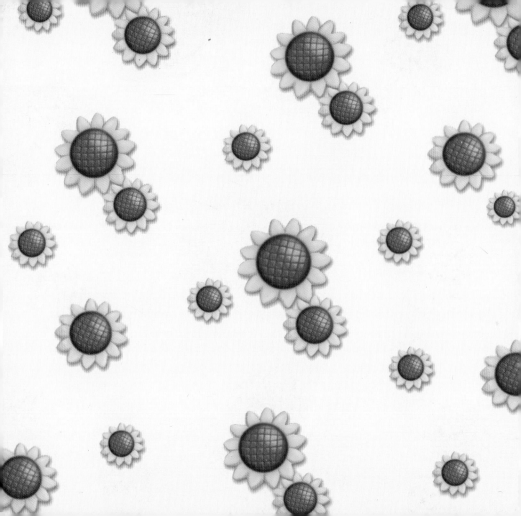

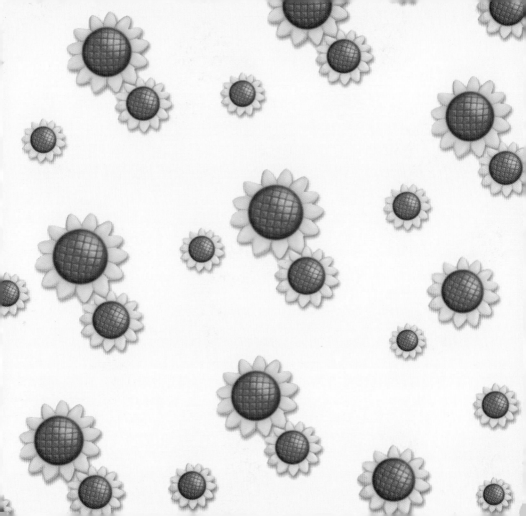

EGMONT

We bring stories to life

First published in Great Britain 2009 by Egmont UK Limited
The Yellow Building,1 Nicholas Road, London W11 4AN

Endpapers and introductory illustrations by Craig Cameron.

HiT entertainment

ISBN 978 1 4052 4628 6

46328/3

Printed in Italy

FSC
www.fsc.org
MIX
Paper from
responsible sources
FSC® C018306

Egmont is passionate about helping to preserve the world's remaining ancient forests.
We only use paper from legal and sustainable forest sources.

This book is made from paper certified by the Forest Stewardship Council® (FSC®),
an organisation dedicated to promoting responsible management of forest resources.
For more information on the FSC, please visit www.fsc.org. To learn more about
Egmont's sustainable paper policy, please visit www.egmont.co.uk/ethical

The lighthouse lamp has broken and Bob's team has to mend it before it gets dark. Can their new team-mate, whose name is Flex, help save the day?

It was a sunny morning down at Bobland Bay and Bob had an important job to do.

"We are going to put up solar panels for the lighthouse today," Bob said to Scoop.

"So the light will keep going, even if there is a power cut!" Scoop replied, excitedly.

"That's right!" Bob smiled. "Now, where's Mr Bell, the lighthouse keeper?"

Just then, Mr Bell appeared from behind the lighthouse. He looked very worried.

"Bob!" he cried. "The lamp in the lighthouse has broken! Can you help?"

"Hmm … Scoop isn't tall enough to reach it," Bob told him. "But there's a new machine coming today. His name is Flex. He'll be perfect for the job!"

"We must fix it before dark," Mr Bell began, "so the ships can keep away from the rocks!"

Meanwhile, the new machine was lost in the woods. "Which way do I go?" cried Flex, whizzing round in a panic. "I'm late!"

Suddenly, he heard voices so he zoomed through an opening in the trees.

"Oh, hello!" said Lofty. "Are you Flex? You've got an arm just like me!"

"Yes! Look, it goes up really high!" said Flex. "And I've got a basket to carry things in."

"Wow, that's really useful!" said Roley.

Just then, Bob rolled in on Scoop and saw Flex showing the machines his arm.

"Hello! You must be Flex," Bob smiled. "Now team, we have lots to do today!"

"The lighthouse lamp is broken," said Scoop. "We've got to put a new one in."

"The new lamp is at the docks," said Bob. "Packer and Lofty, you can go and fetch it."

"Erm, so there's nothing for me to do?" said Flex, looking disappointed.

"Why don't you go, too?" said Wendy. "Packer and Lofty can show you around."

"Oh, yes please!" cried Flex. "I don't want to get lost again."

"Right then, off you go," said Bob. "The rest of the team can come with me to the workshop. We have to fetch the frames for the solar panels. Can we fit them?"

"Yes, we can!" shouted the team.

Packer, Lofty and Flex soon arrived at the docks. They gathered round the lamp.

"Please let me carry it!" begged Flex, waving his arm excitedly. "I'd love to help."

"All right, Flex," said Lofty. "I'll load you up."

Flex set off, carrying the lamp in his basket. "Yippee, look at my bendy arm!" he said, swinging the basket up and down.

"That's great, Flex," Lofty began, "but take care. The lamp is wobbling in your basket."

"Don't worry!" chuckled Flex, swinging his arm. "I'm just giving Packer a break."

"It's *my* job to carry things," grumbled Packer. "Careful, Flex! FLEX! Watch out!"

Suddenly, Flex jolted to a stop. His basket was stuck in a tree! He lowered his arm but the lamp was stuck in the branches.

"Oh no! What have I done?" cried Flex. "My silly bendy arm has made me mess up. Now I'll never be part of the team!"

Back at the lighthouse, Bob and the team were putting the solar panels in place when Mr Bell rushed over to them.

"Has the lamp arrived yet, Bob?" he asked.

Just then, Packer and Lofty raced up. "Just in time!" said Bob. "Have you got the lamp?"

"Er, well, no. It's stuck in a tree," Packer explained, quietly. "Flex had an accident."

"Oh dear!" cried Bob. "Show me where."

Bob and the crew rushed to the woods and set to work getting the lamp down.

"Bob's team don't need me," sniffed Flex.

Lofty tried to lift Bob up but he couldn't reach the lamp. "Where's Flex?" asked Bob. "We need his help to get the lamp out."

"Here I am!" cried Flex. "I can help!"

He lowered his basket and Bob climbed in. Then Flex lifted him high into the trees.

"OK Flex, go right a bit . . . now we need your hook, Lofty. Steady. Got it!" Bob said, as he carefully attached Lofty's hook to the lamp. Raising his hook, Lofty lifted the lamp free.

"We're a great team, Flex!" beamed Lofty.

"Yes, but I've messed up," said Flex, sadly. "Bob won't want me on the team now."

"Don't be silly, Flex!" laughed Bob. "We've got a very important job for you to do."

Back at the lighthouse, Mr Bell was delighted to see Bob and the team.

"We have to get the lamp in place before it gets dark," said Mr Bell.

"Don't worry, Mr Bell," replied Bob. "With Flex to help, we'll get it fixed in no time!"

Bob climbed into Flex's basket with the lamp. Then Flex raised the basket up to the top of the lighthouse. Bob fitted the new lamp just as the sun was setting.

Mr Bell flicked on the switch. The lighthouse beam gleamed across the sea.

"Well done, everyone!" said Wendy.

"I'm sorry I couldn't do the carrying and the lifting, too," said Flex.

"Flex, being in a team means doing what you're best at," said Bob. "With your bendy arm, you're a fantastic new team-mate."

"Hooray for Flex!" everyone cheered.

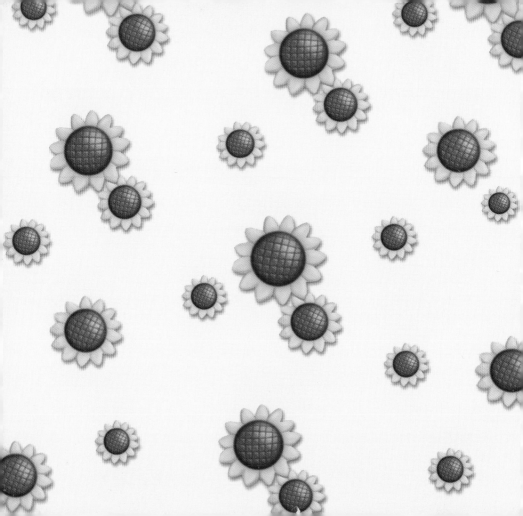